More I Like to Read® Books by
Emily Arnold McCully

Late Nate in a Race
A BANK STREET COLLEGE BEST CHILDREN'S BOOK OF THE YEAR

Little Ducks Go
"It would be easy to believe that the energetic pen-and-watercolor illustrations were sketched from life."
Kirkus Reviews

Pete Won't Eat
★"New readers will eat this up."
Kirkus Reviews (starred review)

★"The illustrations are priceless."
School Library Journal (starred review)

Sam and the Big Kids
"Young kids . . . will relate to Sam's story, cheer Sam's heroism, and delight in their own achievement of reading this title all by themselves."
The Bulletin of the Center for Children's Books

3, 2, I,
Go!

Emily Arnold McCully

I
Like to
Read®

Holiday House / New York

To Ethan

I LIKE TO READ is a registered trademark of Holiday House, Inc.

Copyright © 2015 by Emily Arnold McCully
All Rights Reserved
HOLIDAY HOUSE is registered in the U.S. Patent and Trademark Office.
Printed and Bound in October 2014 at Tien Wah Press, Johor Bahru, Johor, Malaysia.
The artwork was created with pen and ink and watercolor.
www.holidayhouse.com
First Edition
1 3 5 7 9 10 8 6 4 2

Library of Congress Cataloging-in-Publication Data
McCully, Emily Arnold, author, illustrator.
3, 2, 1, go! / by Emily Arnold McCully. — First edition.
    pages cm
ISBN 978-0-8234-3288-2 (hardcover)
[1. Play—Fiction.] I. Title. II. Title: Three, two, one, go!
PZ7.M478415Aae 2015
[E]—dc23
2014013402

ISBN 978-0-8234-3314-8 (paperback)

"Let's play school," said Ann.
"I'll be the teacher."
"Okay," said Bess.

"Oh, no! Here comes Min," said Ann.

"This is a school zone, Min.
School is hard.
You are not ready."

"Here is the line," said Ann.
"You may not step over it."

"Okay. She is gone. Now spell *smart*."

Min rolled a rock.

Then she got a board.

"What is Min doing?" said Bess.
"Don't mind her," said Ann.

"Now count
to 100."

Min got a tube and some rope.

The board went
on the rock.
The tube got
a top.

The tube went on the board.

Trees in rainforests grow close together.

The top layer of trees is called the canopy.

African crowned eagle

Black colobus monkey

Some creatures that live in the canopy never set foot on the forest floor.

African forest elephants

Slender-snouted crocodile

Lots of medicines come from rainforest plants.

Hippopotamus

Some of the world's biggest rivers flow through rainforests.

Butterfly

Lobelia

Gaboon viper

These animals and plants live in rainforests in West Africa.

Broadbills

Mandrills

Goliath beetle

Frozen poles

The North and South Poles are the coldest parts of the planet. The land and sea close to the poles are covered in snow and ice all year.

Research station

Albatross

People don't live on the South Pole, but scientists sometimes visit to do research.

Leopard seal

Killer whale

Emperor penguins huddle together for warmth.

Gentoo penguins

This floating ice has broken off a bigger block called an iceberg.

Weddell seal

The area around the South Pole is covered by a vast stretch of land called Antarctica. Most living things are found on the edge of this land, in or near the sea.

These animals have white fur to blend in with the snow.

Arctic fox

Polar bear

Arctic tern

Puffin

Walrus

Lemming

Reindeer

Both these animals live in water, often under ice.

Narwhal

Gelatinous seasnail

The area around the North Pole is called the Arctic. It's mostly covered by a frozen ocean. Many creatures that live here have a lot of body fat and thick fur to keep warm.

Parka (coat with fur hood)

Snow goggles

Mukluk (watertight boots)

The Inuit people live in the Arctic parts of Canada, Alaska and Greenland.

Some Inuit people build temporary shelters called igloos out of snow.

Mountain high

Mountains are the highest places on Earth.
They're so high, the weather at the bottom, or base, can
be very different from the weather at the top, or peak.

The coldest part of a
mountain is the peak.
Not many things live here.

Mountain
peak

Some mountain peaks
stay cold enough for
snow all year round.

Ski lift

Snow line

Over time, pieces
of rock fall down to
form a scree slope.

The higher slopes
are too cold for
trees to grow.

Scree
slope

Lake

Pine trees

When the snow and ice at the top melt,
they trickle down to form lakes at the base.

In winter, lots of mountains are entirely covered in snow.

In summer, most of the snow melts. Lots of plants and animals come out.

Valley

Near its start, a river is narrow and flows fast.

Rain and melted snow trickle down from steep slopes.

Often two rivers join together.

When a river flows over a steep step, it makes a waterfall.

Wetland

Kayaks

Paddle steamer

As a river widens, it starts to flow more slowly, making giant bends.

Here are some of the creatures that live in rivers.

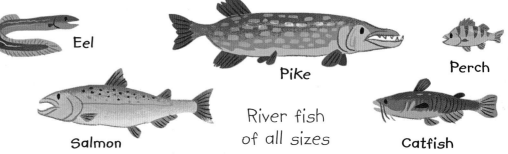

Eel

Pike

Perch

Salmon

River fish of all sizes

Catfish

Running rivers

Even the widest river begins as a narrow stream on a hill.
A river always flows downhill, collecting more water along its way.
It ends when it meets another river, a lake or the sea.

Town

This river ends when it flows into the sea. This is called the mouth.

Reeds

Towards its end, a river can become muddy and shallow.

A river's mouth can be thousands of miles away from its start.

Pelican

Birds with webbed feet or long legs

Heron

Otter

Beaver

Animals with thick fur and strong tails

The coast

The place where land meets the sea is called the coast. Here you might find cliffs, beaches and all sorts of sea life.

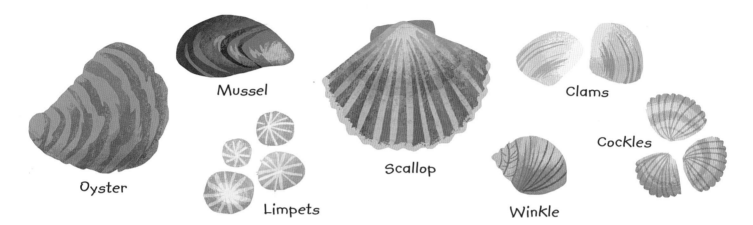

Mussel

Clams

Cockles

Oyster

Limpets

Scallop

Winkle

The seashells that wash up onto the coast are the remains of different sea creatures.

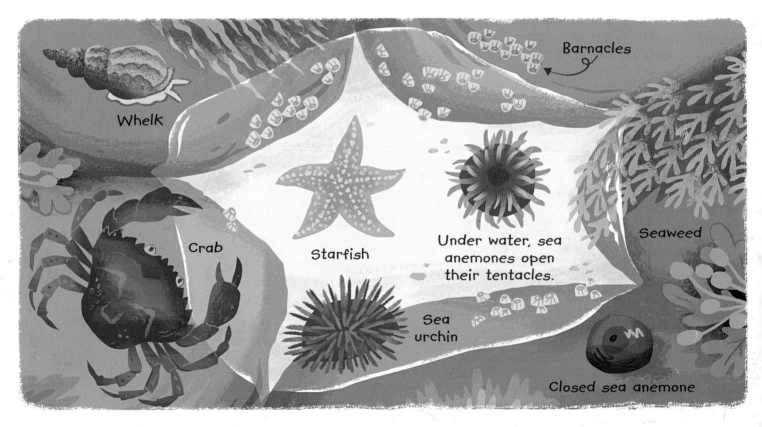

Barnacles

Whelk

Crab

Starfish

Under water, sea anemones open their tentacles.

Seaweed

Sea urchin

Closed sea anemone

Rock pools are left behind when waves wash over the rocks.

When it's dark, lighthouses shine a light to show boats where the cliffs are.

Black-headed gull

Seagulls live and hunt close to the sea.

Nesting fulmars

Herring gull

Cliff face

Headland

Cave

Deck chairs

Crashing waves have helped shape these rocks.

Lifeguards watch people in the water.

Beach umbrella

When it's windy, the waves are bigger and more powerful.

Sailing boat

Seal

Rock pool

Lifeboats look out for other boats or swimmers in trouble.

Buoys show boats where it's safe to pass.

Under the sea

Most of the Earth is covered by salty seawater.
Some sea creatures are found in the deepest,
darkest parts of the ocean, but most live
near the surface, or in shallow seas.

Scuba
diver

Turtles

Jellyfish

A group of fish is
called a shoal.

Sea
anemone

Brain
coral

Stingray

Lionfish

Coral reefs are
found in warm,
shallow waters.

Tree
coral

Staghorn
coral

Giant clam

Sea
snake

Cone shells

Crab

Octopus

A quarter of all sea creatures
live on coral reefs.

The oceans provide food for people all over our world.

Some sea creatures need to come to the surface to breathe.

Scientists travel in underwater ships called submarines to study sea creatures.

Parts of the ocean are so deep that sunlight can't reach the bottom.

Under the ground

The world beneath our feet is full of life
and buzzing with activity, just as it is on the surface.

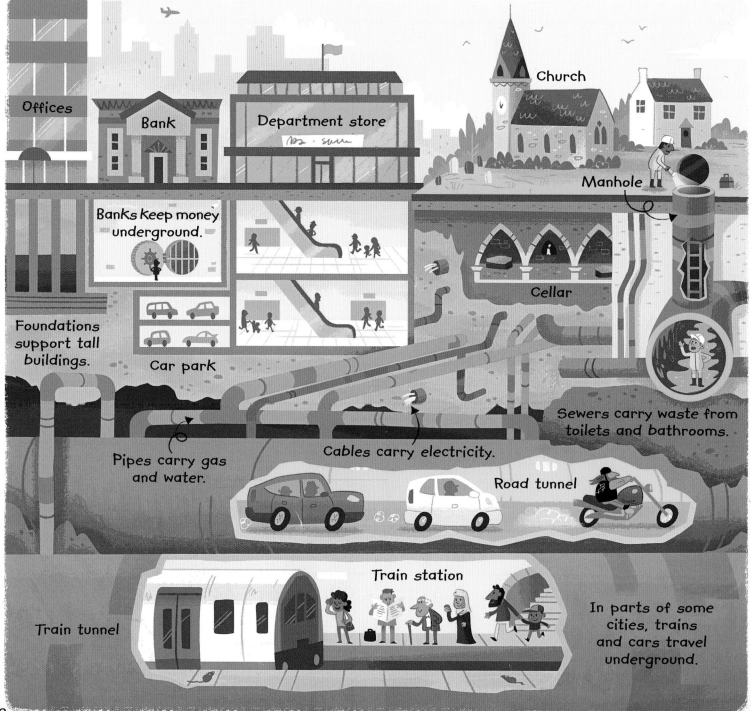

Offices

Bank

Department store

Church

Manhole

Banks keep money underground.

Cellar

Foundations support tall buildings.

Car park

Sewers carry waste from toilets and bathrooms.

Pipes carry gas and water.

Cables carry electricity.

Road tunnel

Train station

Train tunnel

In parts of some cities, trains and cars travel underground.

Lots of creatures live in the soil, near the surface.

Mole

Mole burrow

Ants

Earthworm

Termites

Close-up view of the soil

This hole leads to an underground cave.

Tree roots

Rabbit warren

Animal remains

Layers of soil

Ancient objects

Hold steady!

Underneath the soil, there is solid rock.

Sleeping bats

Stalactites

Stalagmites

Fossil bones

Cave salamanders

Underground river

Without torches, this cave would be completely dark.

23

Wild weather

Storms look different all over the world. The most powerful storms don't happen often, but when they strike, they show the weather at its wildest.

In dry places, dust storms can blow sand for thousands of miles.

In cold parts of the world, blizzards can cover huge areas in thick layers of snow.

Tornadoes are winds that spin around very fast to make funnel-shaped clouds.

Some storms are so big you can even see them from space. They look like huge swirls.

The strongest storms are called hurricanes and typhoons.
They build up over warm seas. When they reach land they can destroy whole towns.

Dark clouds

Lightning is a spark of electricity. It can flash in the sky or strike the ground.

Lightning

KABOOM!

Thunder is the sound caused by lightning. It can be heard from miles away.

Wind can blow down power lines which take electricity to people's homes.

Storm shutters

Broken windows

Fallen trees

Sand bags stop water from coming in under doors.

River

25

Volcanoes

Volcanoes are openings in the Earth's surface. Sometimes the hot sticky rock that's buried deep underneath bursts through, causing a big explosion known as an eruption.

This volcano is erupting.

Clouds of ash

Hot gases

The red-hot rock that's forced out is called lava.

Blocks of solid rock

When lava cools, it becomes solid rock.

Lava

Some lava is runny and flows quickly.
Other lava is lumpy and flows slowly.

Over time, most volcanoes grow
into tall mountains made from
layers of ash and cooled lava.

Crops

Some volcanoes have
stopped erupting.
They're called extinct.

Ash from past eruptions
makes the soil rich. Crops
grow easily here.

Volcanoes under the sea
can grow into islands that
stick up above the water.

THE LAND OF STORIES

A TREASURY OF CLASSIC
FAIRY TALES

A NOTE TO ALL STORYTELLERS

I magine a world with *magic*. Now imagine this place is home to everything and everyone you were told wasn't "real." Imagine it has fairies and witches, mermaids and unicorns, giants and dragons, and trolls and goblins. Imagine they live in places like enchanted forests, gingerbread houses, underwater kingdoms, or castles in the sky.

Personally, I know such a place exists because it's where I'm from. This magical world is not as distant as you think. In fact, you've been there many times before. You travel there whenever you hear the words "Once upon a time." It's another realm, where all your favorite fairy-tale and nursery-rhyme characters live. In your world, we call it *the Land of Stories*.

For those of you familiar with fairy tales, I'm known as the Fairy Godmother. I'm best remembered for transforming Cinderella's raggedy clothes into a beautiful gown for the prince's ball—but I won't give anything else away in case you haven't read it. You'll be delighted to see it's the first story in this treasury.

I understand this all may come as a bit of a surprise. It's not every day you learn that a place like the Land of Stories exists outside one's imagination. Although it shouldn't be *that* shocking if you think about it: After all, if fiction is inspired by mythology, and myths are just embellished legends, and legends are exaggerated history, then *all* stories must have an element of truth to them. And I can assure you that the fairy-tale world is as real as the book you're holding in your hands.

You're probably wondering *how* the stories of the fairy-tale world became so prevalent in your world. Allow me to explain, for I am entirely to blame.

Many centuries ago, I discovered your world by accident. After a long and wonderful career of helping people (like Cinderella) achieve their dreams, I was only eager to do more. So one day I closed my eyes, waved my magic wand, and said, "I wish to go someplace where people need me the most." When I opened my eyes, I was no longer in the Land of Stories.

When I first arrived, your world was enduring a time known as *the Dark Ages*, and there couldn't be a better description. It was a period consumed with poverty, plague, and war. People were suffering and starving, and they were very doubtful that conditions would get any better.

I did what I could to help the people I met: I treated the sick, I fed the hungry, and I even tried to stop the violence throughout the land. Unfortunately, nothing I did prevented the disease and destitution from spreading.

However, it wasn't *interaction* your world needed; it was *inspiration*. In a world dominated by ruthless kings and warlords, the ideas of *self-worth* and *self-empowerment* were unheard of. So I started telling stories about my world to entertain and raise spirits, especially the poor children's. Little did I know it would become the greatest contribution of my lifetime.

I told stories about cowards who became heroes, peasants who became powerful, and the lonely who became beloved. The stories taught many lessons, but most important, they taught the world how to dream. The ability to dream was a much-needed introduction to *hope*, and it spread like a powerful epidemic. Families passed the stories from generation to generation, and over the years I watched their compassion and courage change the world.

I recruited other fairies to help me spread the tales from the Land of Stories around the world, and the stories became known as *fairy tales*. Over time, we asked writers like the Brothers Grimm, Hans Christian Andersen, and Charles Perrault to publish the stories so they would live on forever.

During that time, I realized how important *storytelling* is. While philosophy and science help enhance our mind and body, storytelling stimulates our spirit. It broadens our imagination, teaches us valuable lessons, shows us that things are not always as they seem, and encourages us to reach our greatest potential.

With that said, I have a favor to ask of anyone reading this: *Become a storyteller!* Read to others the fairy tales in this book. Read them stories from another book. If you can, create your own stories to share. When you pass along the art of storytelling to your family and friends, you make the world a better place.

By inspiring someone, you stimulate that person's creativity; and when someone is gifted with creativity, he or she inherently holds the source of *progress* and *prosperity*. Creativity is the simple but powerful ability to make something from nothing, and it just so happens that *making something from nothing* is also the definition of *magic*.

Become a storyteller and help us keep fairy tales alive. Even if people don't believe in magic, never let the world forget what it represents. Wherever there is a storyteller, there will always be hope.

Thank you, and may you all have a *happily-ever-after*!

With love,
The Fairy Godmother

CINDERELLA

ADAPTED FROM
CHARLES PERRAULT

Once upon a time, there was a lovely little girl named Cinderella. She was as beautiful as she was kind and treated everyone with compassion and respect, from the lords and ladies that lived in her village to the small mice that lived in her garden. Cinderella had a heart of gold and was beloved and befriended by all she met.

She lived in a charming home with her mother and father, and they were as happy as a family could be, until the unfortunate day her mother passed away.

Fearing Cinderella would grow up unhappy without a mother, her father soon remarried a widow from the village who had two daughters of her own. Her stepmother wasn't as warm or gentle as Cinderella's mother had been, and her stepsisters weren't very kind, but Cinderella loved them like the family she hoped they'd become.

Sadly, shortly after the marriage began, Cinderella's father also died, leaving her alone with her stepmother and stepsisters. It was then that her new family's true nature revealed itself. They removed everything from the home that had belonged to Cinderella's mother and father and filled the house with their own belongings. The stepsisters took Cinderella's bedroom for themselves and made her sleep on a stack of hay in the cellar. The stepmother took Cinderella's dresses away and gave her raggedy clothes to wear.

"If you want to continue living here, you'll have to work for it," the stepmother said.

From then on, Cinderella wasn't treated like a sister or daughter, but like a maid. Her stepmother and stepsisters gave her grueling chores and frivolous tasks and made her wait on them hand and foot as they enjoyed their new home.

As time went on, Cinderella grew to be a beautiful young woman, igniting the jealousy of her two stepsisters. As punishment for her beauty, they added to her chores until she was constantly covered in dirt, and Cinderella forgot she was pretty at all.

Despite her misfortune, Cinderella remained a kind and compassionate person. She knew her heart of gold was something her stepmother and stepsisters could never take away, and that alone gave her joy on the gloomiest days. She may have spent her time working for her stepfamily, but the nights were hers to dream of a better life, and those dreams gave her hope that good things would come.

One day, royal invitations were sent throughout the kingdom inviting all the young women in the land to a special ball the king and queen were hosting at the palace. At the ball, the very handsome Prince Charming would dance with all the young women in attendance and choose his future bride.

It was the most exciting news the kingdom had heard in years, and Cinderella's house was buzzing with anticipation. For weeks leading up to the ball, Cinderella's stepmother and stepsisters spoke of nothing else. The stepsisters took turns fantasizing about what it would be like to dance with the prince and accept his marriage proposal. They purchased elegant fabrics and ordered Cinderella to make them dresses for the occasion.

While she listened to her stepsisters' daydreams and sewed their dresses, Cinderella also dreamed of what it would be like to attend the ball. She had never been to the palace before and wanted nothing more than to attend the ball with the other young women of the kingdom. When she was little she'd loved listening to her father's stories about visiting the palace on special occasions. He had promised to take her there one day when she was older, but now that he was gone, the ball seemed like Cinderella's only chance.

Cinderella worked on her stepsisters' dresses around the clock, hoping she would finish with enough time to make something for herself to wear. Soon the night of the ball came, and Cinderella only had time to sew patches over the holes and tears of her raggedy clothes.

A carriage arrived to take the stepmother and stepsisters to the palace, and Cinderella followed them outside.

"Where do you think you're going?" the stepmother asked.

"To the ball, of course," Cinderella said.

"You can't go to the palace dressed in those hideous rags," the stepmother said.